W9-AFX-407

ZPL

WITHDRAWN

CREATIVE

A Busy Week

A humorous
rhyming story

This edition first published in 2006 by
Sea-to-Sea Publications
1980 Lookout Drive
North Mankato
Minnesota 56003

Text © Sue Graves 2004, 2006
Illustration © Melanie Sharp 2004

Printed in China

All rights reserved

Library of Congress Cataloging-in-Publication Data:

Graves, Sue.
  A busy week / by Sue Graves.
    p.cm. — (Reading corner)
  Summary: A young girl helps members of her family perform various tasks throughout
the week, with unexpected results.
  ISBN 1-59771-005-9
  [1. Helpfulness-—Fiction. 2. Family life—Fiction. 3. Stories in rhyme.] I. Title. II. Series.

PZ8.3.S7426Bu2005
[E]—dc22

                                                                    2004063631

9 8 7 6 5 4 3 2

Published by arrangement with the Watts Publishing Group Ltd, London

Series Editor: Jackie Hamley
Series Advisors: Linda Gambrell, Dr. Barrie Wade, Dr. Hilary Minns
Design: Peter Scoulding

A Busy Week

Written by
Sue Graves

Illustrated by
Melanie Sharp

SEA-TO-SEA
Mankato   Collingwood   London

Hussey-Mayfield Memorial
Public Library
Zionsville, IN 46077

Sue Graves
"I have four children and two cats so my house is very noisy! I teach children and love writing books. I hope you enjoy this one!"

Melanie Sharp
"I love to draw because it lets you have fun with your imagination. Happy reading!"

On Monday I helped Mom
to wash the kitchen floor.

6

On Tuesday I helped Bert
to mend the garage door.

9

11

On Wednesday I helped
Gran to bake an apple pie.

12

14

15

On Thursday I helped Raj
to build his tower high.

17

19

On Friday I helped Dad
to fix the bathroom leak.

And so today, I'll stay in bed.
I've had a busy week!

23

Notes for parents and teachers

READING CORNER has been structured to provide maximum support for new readers. The stories may be used by adults for sharing with young children. Primarily, however, the stories are designed for newly independent readers, whether they are reading these books in bed at night, or in the reading corner at school or in the library.

Starting to read alone can be a daunting prospect. READING CORNER helps by providing visual support and repeating words and phrases, while making reading enjoyable. These books will develop confidence in the new reader, and encourage a love of reading that will last a lifetime!

If you are reading this book with a child, here are a few tips:

1. Make reading fun! Choose a time to read when you and the child are relaxed and have time to share the story.

2. Encourage children to reread the story, and to retell the story in their own words, using the illustrations to remind them what has happened.

3. Give praise! Remember that small mistakes need not always be corrected.

READING CORNER covers three grades of early reading ability, with three levels at each grade. Each level has a certain number of words per story, indicated by the number of bars on the spine of the book, to allow you to choose the right book for a young reader:

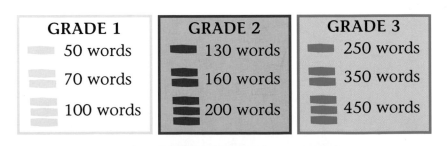

GRADE 1	GRADE 2	GRADE 3
50 words	130 words	250 words
70 words	160 words	350 words
100 words	200 words	450 words

06/10